# The Littles
## and the
## Scary Halloween

# The Littles
## and the
## Scary Halloween

*Adapted by* **Teddy Slater**
*from* **THE LITTLES AND THE**
 **GREAT HALLOWEEN SCARE**
*by* **John Peterson**
*Illustrated by* **Jacqueline Rogers**

SCHOLASTIC INC.
New York  Toronto  London  Auckland  Sydney
Mexico City  New Delhi  Hong Kong  Buenos Aires

Every Halloween, Tom and Lucy
Little tried to scare their parents.
But Mr. and Mrs. Little were
hard to scare.

When you're less than
six inches tall
from head to tail,
you have to be brave.

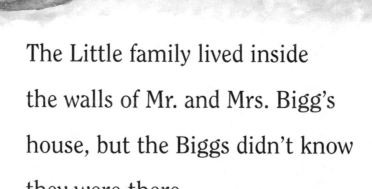

The Little family lived inside
the walls of Mr. and Mrs. Bigg's
house, but the Biggs didn't know
they were there.

As brave as they were,

the Littles were careful

to keep it that way.

Tom and Lucy spent days
trying to come up with a
scary new trick for Halloween.
But by Halloween morning
they still didn't have a plan.

"Let's go up to the attic,"

Tom whispered to Lucy.

"It's nice and creepy there.

It's the perfect place

to think of scary things."

Lucy thought the attic was

a bit *too* creepy.

But she didn't want Tom

to think *she* wasn't brave.

The Littles had their own elevator

made from a tin can.

It went up and down inside the walls.

Tom pulled the ropes

and the elevator took them

up, up — all the way to the attic.

"Wow!" Tom cried.
"There must be lots
of stuff we can use
to scare Mom and Dad."

"This stuff sure scares me!" Lucy said.

Tom headed for a

dark corner.

"I'll look here," he said.

"Lucy, you look there."

A few minutes later
Tom heard a scream.
He raced toward
the sound.

Lucy was trapped!

And a big hairy spider was

creeping her way.

Tom saw a pin on the floor.

He picked it up and faced

the spider.

The spider looked back at Tom

with beady red eyes. Then...

...it turned around and ran away.

"Oh, Tom," Lucy cried. "You saved my life."

"YUCK!" Tom cried.

"This spiderweb is sticky!"

The Littles took the elevator
down to the Biggs' kitchen.
They washed off the cobwebs.
Just then, they heard a noise.
Mrs. Bigg was coming!

"Quick, hide!" Tom whispered.

"We will wait in here

until Mrs. Bigg leaves."

But Mrs. Bigg did not leave.

She put on an apron

and began to make a pumpkin pie.

Tom and Lucy waited
and waited.
And while they waited,
they nibbled on the sweet,
ripe pumpkin.

All that waiting and nibbling

made them sleepy.

Finally, they curled up

and fell asleep.

Meanwhile, Mr. and Mrs. Little
were very worried.
So were Uncle Pete and Granny.
Tom and Lucy had disappeared!

The Littles searched all over.

But there was no sign

of Tom or Lucy.

Mrs. Little began to cry.

"Where are they?" she sobbed.

"They've been missing

since breakfast."

Suddenly, the Biggs' clock struck noon.

The sound of the clock

woke Tom and Lucy.

They stood up and peeked out.

The pie was cooling on the
counter, and Mrs. Bigg
was nowhere to be seen.

Tom and Lucy hopped out

of the pumpkin...dashed across the counter...

and through a secret opening

to the Littles' apartment.

Mrs. Little wiped away her tears.

"Tom! Lucy!" she cried.

"What a fright you gave us.

We thought something terrible

had happened to you."

Tom and Lucy hugged

their parents.

"We're sorry," Lucy said.

"We didn't mean to scare you that much."

Tom winked at Lucy.

"Not *this* time..." he said.

"But just wait until next year!"